HOLLY KELLER

Lizzie's Invitation

GREENWILLOW BOOKS, NEW YORK

First Edition   10 9 8 7 6 5 4 3 2 1

The full-color illustrations are watercolor.
The text type is Weidemann Book.

Library of Congress Cataloging-in-Publication Data
Keller, Holly.
Lizzie's invitation.
Summary: Lizzie is upset that she did not
receive a party invitation until she meets Amanda
who also was not invited to the party, and
they have a fine afternoon playing together.
[1. Disappointment—Fiction.
2. Friendship—Fiction]   I. Title.
PZ7.K28132Li 1987   [E]   86-19380
ISBN 0-688-06124-9
ISBN 0-688-06125-7 (lib. bdg.)

FOR ANNA ROSE LAWRENCE

AND HER PARENTS

Alex got one and Loren got one.
Tommy got one, too. Lizzie knew because she
could see it sticking out of his back pocket.

The envelopes were blue with
yellow balloons on the front.

They were invitations to a birthday party.
Kate gave them out at lunchtime, and
Lizzie didn't get one.

Lizzie took some carrot sticks out of her
lunch box and went over to Kate.
"Want some carrots, Kate?" she asked. Lizzie
hoped Kate still had an envelope for her.

"Sure," Kate said. "Want some raisins?"
"OK," Lizzie said.
    Then Kate walked away and
    sat with Tommy.

Lizzie took her lunch box behind
the easel and ate by herself.
The peanut butter tasted funny.

She painted a picture of angry yellow faces.
"No happy faces today?" Mrs. Healy asked.
Lizzie just shrugged.

The next day Lizzie didn't want to go to school.
"Don't you feel well?" Mama asked. Lizzie shook
her head, and Mama put her into bed for a rest.

Lizzie made a birthday card for Kate, but she
threw it away. She had a party for her dolls,
but it wasn't any fun. So she went to sleep.

Saturday was the day of Kate's party.
It was raining and Lizzie felt sad.

After breakfast she put on her raincoat
and went outside.
"Don't stay out too long," Mama said.

Lizzie walked down the street to the
playground. The swings were all wet,
and the sandbox was muddy.

She squatted down and watched a leaf float in
a puddle. She could see her face in the water.

Then there was another face.
"Hi," the other face said.

Lizzie stood up to see who was there. It was
Amanda, a girl in her class.
"Want to try the see-saw?" Amanda asked.
Lizzie didn't really feel like it, but she said OK.

The see-saw made a creaky sound.

Then Amanda
bumped Lizzie,
and Lizzie
bumped Amanda.
Lizzie laughed.
They made
big splashes
in the puddles
with their feet.

Amanda giggled.
"My socks are all wet."
"Mine too," Lizzie said.

"Can you come over to my house?"
  Amanda asked.
"Aren't you going to Kate's party?"
  Lizzie asked.
"No," Amanda said, "I wasn't invited."
"Me either," Lizzie said.
  And they didn't talk about it anymore.

Amanda's mother gave Lizzie a pair of slippers
to wear while her socks were drying.
They were *very* big.

Then she called Lizzie's mother to say
that Lizzie was staying to play.

There was vegetable soup for lunch. Amanda
liked to put crackers in her soup, too.

After lunch, they played
with Amanda's dress-up clothes.

Lizzie helped Amanda make
curtains for her doll house,

When it was time for Lizzie to leave, Amanda
walked outside with her to say goodbye.
"I had a good time," Lizzie said.
"Me too," Amanda said.

"See you Monday at school," Amanda called
when Lizzie got to the end of the path.
Lizzie waved and took a cookie out of the
bag to eat on the way home.

and they made pictures with their
fingers on the foggy windows.

Amanda showed Lizzie how to make jelly cookies.
"The grape ones are the best," Amanda said,
and she put some in a bag for Lizzie
to take home.